GALAHAD, KNIGHT ERRANT

GALAHAD

GALAHAD
KNIGHT ERRANT

By

MAY E. SOUTHWORTH

BOSTON: RICHARD G. BADGER
The Gorham Press
MCMVII

ISBN-10: 0991560620
ISBN-13: 978-0-9915606-2-2

Cavalier Books

To

JAMES ROBINSON STUDLEY

the inspiration of

achievement

THE ALLEGORY

THE ALLEGORY

THE beautiful and spiritual symbolism of the Holy Grail, whatever its source or tradition, has been woven in ballad and story for so many centuries that it has now taken a permanent place in legendary history and is acknowledged to be one of the world's most fascinating romances. Through the various picturesque stories of adventure and chivalry abounding in religious mysticism, there is always one perfect knight striving towards the goal, pure and unselfish, who through loving service to others, and a life of absolute purity, finds the highest joy on earth and gains a crown in heaven. Fact and legend, taken from simple beginnings, are so blended and interwoven in this beautiful allegory, that to separate them or analyze the symbolism destroys the exquisite beauty of the romance to one who dearly loves a story.

The experiences of this ideal knight, the difficulties he encounters in conquering sin, the temptations which beset him on every side and his final triumph over all, will never cease to charm, and they belong to all places, all time and every age. Its

9

allegory, the evolution of a character in the pursuit of all good and the developing of the divine which glows pure and perfect within every human soul, is an inspiration to fight the good fight oneself with a set purpose and to strive to live for the abiding good of all, leaving the world better for the effort.

Gleaning from the various Grail heroes, the comparative modern and favorite crusade of Galahad, boy and knight, in quest of this mysterious symbol, seems best to typify to the would-be knight of today the struggles of the human heart in seeking the Great Treasure and reveals best how by a life of purity, a purity with a full knowledge of both good and evil, it is possible to have the strength to overcome the bad and the grace to remain unsullied.

"My strength is the strength of ten because my heart is pure"

THE LEGEND

AS the old legend is told it relates how, when Lucifer was hurled from heaven for his presumption, he lost from the beautiful crown which the angels had given him the largest and brightest gem. This precious stone fell to earth, and from it was fashioned with mysterious and significant care a beautiful cup, which later was set in a standard of pure gold. Veronica, the holy woman who wiped the dust and blood from our Saviour's face with her veil when he was on the way to Calvary, and which miraculously took the impression of His face, brought this gem-like vase to the disciples in the upper chamber, to be used on that Thursday night of the Last Supper where was instituted the office of the Holy Communion.

Joseph of Arimathea was one of the band of faithful apostles and was given this consecrated cup. Having touched the lips of our Lord, he treasured it as the most sacred thing on earth. The next day was the sorrowful tragedy of the crucifixion, and Joseph carried this cup with him to Calvary, and there as night fell and they were allowed to take the

13

Broken Body from the cross, he reverently caught in it the few drops of precious blood which bled afresh from the cruel spear wound in His side.   This sacred vessel now holding the bodily blood of Our Saviour became the Holy Grail and possessed the Christ's own miraculous powers.

On the third day after the crucifixion, the Lord having vanquished death by rising again, the Jews accused Joseph of Arimathea of having stolen the Body and cast him into prison with the intention of starving him to death.   But he had the sacred cup with him which from its wondrous substance fed him physically and so comforted him that he hardly realized the lapse of time which he passed in this dungeon.

After being imprisoned for forty-two years he was finally set at liberty and devoted the remainder of his life to the spread of Christianity.

Undergoing much labor and tribulation, he later came to Britain and brought the Holy Dish with him, which had proved a blessing and even a benediction on the land that held it.   Here he built on a high hill a most beautiful temple all of gold and precious stones expressly to hold it.   The gleaming cup was kept here for generations, guarded night and day by knights appointed and commanded by the king. These Knights of the Temple were the flower and chivalry of the land, as only those who led an absolutely pure life in thought, word and deed were permitted to even protect this sacred relic.

It remained in this strong castle under the authority of Joseph of Arimathea and guarded by his knights as long as he lived and under his descendants successively until it came to the charge of Amfortas, the eighth of his line, called the Fisher-King. Under some evil enchantment this brave king, loyal and righteous in most things, sinned and was false to the sacred trust. Immediately the wrath of heaven fell upon his wickedness. In a flash he was cursed with an incurable disease, and he and his whole court were cast under a trance-like spell and doomed to remain this way and not even be allowed to die until a knight should come to rescue the Holy Grail from this desecrated castle. This same knight must be so pure, so tender of heart and so full of divine pity at the desolation he would see about the court that he would be irresistibly moved to ask the afflicted king the cause of this sinful state and of his own suffering. This service of heartfelt sympathy and love on the part of the knight would instantly free the aged king from this living death and make possible a true death for which he longed, and deliver all the sorrowful company from their hateful bondage.

Although the Grail still abode in the castle, no one there was permitted to see it owing to the curse that lay over all. When the true knight should come who was destined to recover the treasure from this house of sin, it was ordained that the gleaming Grail, covered with a veil of red samite, should pass before his vision in procession attended by angelic maidens, and that part of his question to the king should be to explain this mystery also, and in accomplishing this end bring salvation to all mankind.

*"Love melts away all selfishness
and teaches us the joy of service"*

THE QUEST

ON an Easter morning in the days when Arthur was king of Britain a wonderful child was born to Elaine of the ancient race of David. He was christened Galahad, which signifies purity, as he came into the world destined for a great career and was set apart from his birth for the accomplishment of his mission. To this end, he was given into the keeping of the holy nuns in his infancy, to be cared for by them and brought up in their simple life of abstinence and poverty. When he was but a tiny babe a heavenly vision came to him which seemed to reveal the secret of his future career and the high destiny for which he was born. It came one evening as one of the nuns was soothing him to sleep with a low crooning song and walking back and forth in the dormitory. A shimmering cloud of white drapery fell in front of them, the brightness radiating from a chalice borne in the hands of an angel over which poised a white dove swinging from his beak a golden censor. The nun fell on her knees in adoration, but the cup gleamed and quivered with such dazzling radiance through its thin covering, that she was obliged to turn away, screening her face with the babe. But he, laughing fearlessly in eager delight at its brightness stretches out his tiny arms, reaching up as if to grasp the sacred emblem, whose light with its spiritual power is destined to be his guiding star through life.

As he grew to boyhood in the seclusion of the convent, for amusement he learned to make for himself arrows, and with his bow thoughtlessly shot them at the little birds and the tiny squirrels as they flitted among the forest where he was permitted to play. But one day as he lay stretched at length on a mossy bank, his ears filled with the joyous songs of the happy birds, and watching the merry frolic of the gentle squirrels darting from the ground to the trees, it came to him that in so carelessly taking the mystery of their sweet lives he was committing a cruel sin. His heart swelled with sorrow for his selfish sport, and he reached out in anger, snapping his bow in two, vowing never again to shed innocent blood, but to tenderly care for all God's little dependent creatures and love every living thing.

As the years passed, and their foster-child became a stalwart youth, strong of arm and straight of limb, restless for things beyond, the nuns realized that the time had come for their noble charge, who had grown so close to their hearts, to go out from their care. His education as far as they were concerned was finished, and he must go forth into the world to be taught in worldly wisdom and manly accomplishments, so as to be invulnerable in arms as well as inviolable to sin and temptation.

He was taken to the military governor and severely trained in horse-back exercise, hunting, wrestling and all things that would make him strong in knightly tournaments. In conduct he was admonished to carry himself with dignity and gravity and to look carefully into all things but to ask few questions. So this pure and honorable young man was educated and fully equipped in all that makes a true knight, ready for the holy adventure when his ancestor, Joseph of Arimathea, should come in his garb of a white hermit to seek him out and present him at the court of king Arthur.

At this time king Arthur was established at Camelot with his famous Round Table, consisting of the noblest fellowship and truest knighthood ever seen together on this earth.

Merlin, the king's friend and counselor, had received tidings that Amfortas, the keeper of the Grail castle, and all his court, lay under an evil spell, and that the holy cup under this magic had mysteriously disappeared. He sent word to king Arthur of his news, advising him at the same time to select some of his worthy knights of the Round Table to undertake the recovery of this sacred relic. The king was pondering this great problem in his heart and wondering how and by whom it could be accomplished, knowing well that this holy adventure could only be achieved by the one stainless hero able to occupy without danger to himself the vacant seat at his table.

This "Siege Perilous" was on the right of the king and nearest to him. It was a seat, perilous for good or evil, and which had long been empty, waiting for the perfect knight without spot or blemish who was ordained to come and hold it without risk to himself. All about the arms and back of the chair was carved in plain letters that lent themselves to the curves, and which ran in and out of the raised figures, these words — "If he who would presume to take this seat be not pure in heart, without fear or reproach he will surely die." To those, who by misadventure had sat there in the years past, it had proven death, so it had been covered with a silken cloth to prevent further mistakes, waiting for the one to arrive so confident in his own integrity that he would take it of his own will fearlessly. It soon happened that on the night of the vigil of Pentecost as the king and all the knights were making merry at the Round Table with delicate viands and fragrant wine, the doors which opened without, flew wide apart of their own volition, letting in a flood of light which filled the grand hall with a radiance brighter than the brightest day. In this dazzling glory came a very aged man, clad all in the white garment of a hermit and so closely cowled that they could only see the tip of his long white beard, and leading by the hand a fair and stately young man.

Awe and curiosity thrilled all the goodly company as the aged hermit slowly traversing the full length of the hall paused at the foot of the throne and said:—

"Sire, I bring you a youth of kingly lineage, brave and innocent, who is worthy of a seat at your table and by whom the quest of the lost Grail can venture to enterprise."

The king rose from his seat and called the comely youth to his side, and as Galahad knelt before him with bared head, he said: —

"I thank God right heartily. Take him, Sire Hermit, to the vacant seat and try if he be by virtue the rightful occupant destined for the holy crusade."

Fearlessly the old hermit led the golden-haired stranger straight to the perilous seat, to the dismay of all the knights, and lifting the covering of silk there gleamed out in wavering letters of golden light over the back of it: —

"This is the seat of Galahad, the Good Knight."

As the graceful youth took the seat, so dangerous to the false and so full of responsibility to the one for whom it was destined, king Arthur said: —

"God make him a good knight, for certainly beauty faileth him not."

The knights all hailed his advent with joy, raising their swords in greeting yet in their hearts they marveled greatly, but bravely said; —

"This surely must be he, for he sits unharmed."

After Galahad had been acknowledged the rightful owner of the "Siege Perilous" and taken the oath of the Round Table, — that is, to be true and loyal in all things to God and the king, — he spent the rest of the night alone in the chapel in holy vigil, feeling that the time was all too short for the preparation of the morning.

With the dawn came two of the best and bravest of king Arthur's knights,— the noble Sir Launcelot and the faithful Sir Bors, — to swear him to the oath of the knights who serve. Kneeling on the high steps of the altar, he took the solemn vows of chivalry, the pledge or covenant to always speak the truth, to maintain the right under all circumstances, to practice kindness and courtesy with all, never to refuse aid to any who are in trouble or need, to succor the orphan and widow, and to maintain his honor in the cause of God in every adventure. The two older knights, kneeling on the steps below, buckled on the young man's heel the golden spur of knighthood and clothed him in a soft red garment covered with an armor of golden chain. Marking his empty scabbard, they took him to the river and showed him a great floating rock shaped like an altar, in which was imbedded a sword with a jeweled hilt.

This marvelous stone, with the sword standing in it, had been a source of great wonderment to all. Not one of the knights or even the king had been able to remove the sword from its rocky bed. But when they bade Galahad try his strength, he withdrew it easily and placed it in the sheath at his side, which fitted it exactly.

He had a beautiful white horse, but as yet was without a shield, but God in His providence had provided him with that also, and it was only necessary that he claim his own.

Behind an altar in an abbey not far from Camelot hung a beautiful white shield, bearing on its face a bright-red cross. This shield had been forged for the heathen Saracen king Evelac whom Joseph of Arimathea had converted to Christianity. As Joseph lay dying he called for this shield and painted on it the brilliant cross with his own blood, bequeathing it to the one who would be the last of his race and who would come to claim it. After Joseph's death it was hung in the abbey, where it had remained all these years, keeping as fresh as when first painted, waiting for the coming of Galahad, who was the last of the kingly house of Joseph of Arimathea. Galahad took possession of the shield and slipping his arm through the band, was now fully equipped for the holy war and adventure, and bound to be invulnerable as long as he wore these mystic arms.

On the morning that the quest of the Holy Grail was to be instituted, the king and all the splendid brotherhood in glittering armor, with silken banners flying, marched in solemn procession to the cathedral to witness the ceremony of king Arthur laying his sword on young Galahad in knighthood, and to be present at the benediction of the bishop on the holy quest. After the knighting of Galahad, he, with the two others chosen for the quest, Sir Launcelot and Sir Bors, stepped forward and kissing the cross, took the oath to "search the wide world over and know no rest until the lost cup is recovered." Amid the blessings of the priests and bishop and the waving banners of their brother-knights bidding them "joy and good adventure," the three pilgrims start out on their holy errand, separately, each taking the direction he likes best, knowing though all can strive, it is only one who will bring the Grail back to the world.

Galahad mounts his white steed, armed with sanctified sword and shield, which seem to guide him from the start to the very goal of his quest,—had he but known it, the abiding place of the Grail.

He rode hard all day, taking refuge and rest at night before the closed door of a chapel. On the evening of the second day he came to a solitary castle set in the midst of a barren and desolate country. All is so quiet and deserted that it seems like the abode of the dead. But Galahad, weary and hungry, finding the drawbridge down, sets spurs to his horse and asks at the entrance gate hospitality for the night. On entering he is met by a dumb servitor who removes his coat of mail and throws over his shoulders a long red mantle. Silently they proceed to a great hall in the center of which is a high couch on which lies a feeble old man gaunt and pallid from a bleeding wound in his thigh. This is the afflicted Fisher-King Amfortas, and the people scattered about in various attitudes are the enchanted court who are waiting in an agony of longing for the coming of the "Good Knight" who is to lift them out of this death-like existence.

Galahad enters like a breath of fresh air in this oppressive silence, rousing the king who moves restlessly on his sick bed as if wakened out of a sleep; and all about the drowsy company of knights, ladies, priests, soldiers and courtiers turn to him with appealing eyes as if a thrill of hope had penetrated the gloom of their dismal enchantment. Galahad gazes mystified and wondering at what he sees about him, but suddenly his roving eyes are caught above and beyond the ailing king and his trance-bound court, to where in the distance he witnesses the wonderful procession of the Sacred Mysteries which the doomed court are not permitted to see. In the beautiful ceremonial which passes, the gleaming cup suffused in soft light and the seven-branched candlestick are carried by lovely maidens, while the bleeding lance is held aloft by noble knights.

Now had Galahad been moved by divine pity at all this misery which he saw about him, and asked the question trembling on his lips as to why the king should suffer so, and to explain the wonderful mystery of the holy procession, he would have released the striken king from his long durance, the whole court from their dream-like existence and ended his own quest; in thus saving others he would also have saved himself. But in pride and assurance he was silent, letting this golden opportunity pass. Not wilfully selfish, but mindful of his too worldly instruction "to think much and speak little," he was overconfident of being able to solve the problem by himself. He was also still lacking in that true brotherly love and compassion which without thought or hesitation takes misery by the hand and gives itself in service.

So he turns, seemingly unmoved and wholly unconscious of his great renunciation, to the next room, where he is invited to sit at the great tables which are spread as for a banquet. He is sumptuously served with the food he likes best, given drink from a golden goblet and shown every attention, but in a hushed and unnaturally quiet manner. Meanwhile the weary king has sunken down on his couch in despair, and the doomed court drawing a stifled breath as if life almost within their grasp had failed them, have gradually fallen back into their hopeless apathy.

When the weary guest had finished eating and drinking, a page showed him to a luxuriant bedchamber, where his courteous host seemed to have neglected nothing for his comfort.

In the morning when he wakened he found every-thing changed as by magic. The room seemed strangely empty and silent, and no answer came to his repeated calls. So putting on his coat of mail, which he found carefully laid by his bed-side, he goes down to the great hall, which was so brilliant with light and full of company the night before, but is now deserted. Not a soul or sign of life about. He goes on through the empty court-yard without meeting anyone, but finds at the entrance gate his horse standing saddled and bridled ready for the journey. He silently mounts, and as the ringing hoofs echo through the strangely desolate air, an oppressive heaviness and dissatisfaction weighs on his conscience. He does not understand exactly how, but knows that he has failed someway in this his first great test,— selfishly accepting much and making no return.

Wrapped in his own gloomy thoughts, he rides slowly on, but is suddenly roused by a wail of anguish which comes from the roadside at his feet. He reins in his steed and is confronted by three very disagreeable elfish faces peering from red hoods. He knows these to be the Loathely Maiden and her two disconsolate companions; beings who for the sin they have wrought in the world have been stripped of all personal charm and transformed into hideous hags. They have recognized Sir Galahad by his shield as the "Good Knight," and as they too

are waiting for the recovery of the Grail to be released
from their loathsome servitude, they question him
in regard to his adventure.   When he tells them that
he has already been to the enchanted castle and
witnessed all the suffering and all the mysteries
there revealed without having spoken, they revile
him and shame him for his heartless dullness:—

"Bad — Heart!" say they.   " Such pity ought to
have risen in thy soul thou couldst not help asking
the question.   Remorse will now dwell in thy heart,
gnawing day and night with bitter pain."

Heaping reproaches on his head, the Loathely
Maiden tells him of his awful mistake, and that in
failing in this opportunity of love and service he has
not only left the court to languish in sin and misery,
but condemned her and her two companions to still
roam the world doing harm and all kinds of wickedness until they be set free.

Humbled and sorrowful he bears their male-
dictions with a heavy heart, thinking to return at
once to the castle, and this time, knowing all he must
do for the afflicted king, feels that he will not be
lacking in that blessed virtue which is to heal him.
But when he turned to go back he found the enchanted castle had dropped out of sight like the
setting sun, and no trace of it could he find.   Up and
down, back and forth, faster and faster he rides in
a rage of disappointment.   He cannot even find
where it stood on that bleak hill.   At last his strength

is spent, and he is obliged to give it up as hopeless and throws himself in anguish to the earth, moaning in agony over the galling memory of his failure. His one effort in life now will be to wipe out this terrible mistake, and until he succeeds the haunting memory of all that waiting suffering will be with him every moment. Strengthened by this sorrowful lesson, he made a vow that in the future he would grapple hand to hand with any misery or misfortune he might come across. By this resolve the burden of his regret is somewhat lightened, and with a more cheerful heart he resumes his wandering quest.

Soon he came to a big black castle with deep ditches dug all around it and enclosed in a thick black wall with high ramparts. Meeting an old dwarf by the way, he asked him if he could tell him the name of this gloomy looking place.

"That, Fair Sir," said the dwarf, "is a cursed castle for the mischief that lies within. It is called the Castle of the Maidens for there they devour many maids."

"All know," said Sir Galahad, "of the Castle of the Maidens and of the seven Knights of Darkness who guard the gates defying the world."

"Then," said the old man, "keep this side, for there is nothing but death for you there."

These seven proprietors of the Black Castle, in revenge for the one fair maiden who had refused their love successively, captured every damsel who passed this way and kept her a prisoner. Here the company, growing larger day by day, languished without a glimmer of hope unless death came to their release. The fame of these wicked knights and their cruel practices had spread throughout the land, and Galahad, unmindful of the old dwarf's cautious counsel, determined that they should be destroyed. Dismounting, he buckled on his armor afresh, tightened his invincible shield more firmly on his arm, and proceeded to the black gate. He was met by the seven brutal knights, who barred his further entrance; so Galahad put forth his sword and smote the foremost to the earth. Then the others charged upon him, but he fought them so hard, and with such desperation, gaining inch by inch, that they were finally completely overcome. Weakened and covered with wounds, they turned and fled.

Galahad could now pass the outer gate, but he found the door within guarded by an aged man in the garb of a monk. Doffing his helmet, he knelt to the *religieuse*, who gave him his blessing and delivered to him the keys, which opened all the doors in the castle. As he turned the key which liberated the fair prisoners, they rushed at him with delight, covering his hands with their grateful kisses, calling him their "Deliverer" and imploring heaven to bless him for his kindly act. He threw wide all the doors of the dark castle, letting in the sunshine and giving liberty not only to the young maid who was the cause of all this trouble, but also to all her innocent associates, who returned to the world and lived happy lives of usefulness ever after.

Galahad set out again with renewed spirits; having vanquished the barbarous knights forever and won in a fight for a good cause, he was tasting the joy which comes in giving a loving service to the unfortunate.

For long, weary months he rode seeking the lost castle, meeting with adventure after adventure, fighting boldly for the right, always conquering and leaving peace and happiness where he had found cruelty and wickedness. His many experiences and his own disappointment had taught him the great need of the tender human sympathy which brother gives to brother, and he felt sure that if now a second opportunity should come to him in the enchanted castle he would not fail or shrink from his duty. The humiliating memory of his weakness in that great test had been his strength in many a battle.

Meanwhile he met the Lady Blanchefleur, dainty and beautiful as the white flower of womanly purity, and embodying all that makes divine womanhood. He wooed and married her, but at the very altar a vision of the Grail came to him which filled his soul as no earthly pleasure could, and he realized that in order to gain this prize for the world and be worthy of his higher purpose he must sacrifice even this wedded love. He had been consecrated to a holy cause, and the flowery chains of love ought to have no power to hold him against those of heaven. Testifying to his vows the gentle bride sadly took the white wreath from her fair braids and bravely lifted her sweet face and bade him "God-speed" making this her sacrifice that his soul might grow to perfection unsullied by worldly ties.

With a heart made more tender by his love and renunciation, he left his sweet wife, the Lady Blanche-fleur, at the altar steps to resume his quest. The thought of the many who through his lack of love and wisdom were left to suffer until his coming again gave him joy in offering up this earthly love that he might be more worthy of the great attainment.

Again he wanders through the barren and sin-stricken country, fighting, if the chance came, and victoriously redeeming many wrongs, his golden armor battered and bearing the scars of many conflicts.

Days, weeks and months he rode through the deep leafless woods and over barren hills, almost discouraged, when one day, after riding far and meeting no one, just as night was falling, he suddenly saw dimly before his tired eyes a faint glimmer of the sad and deserted castle standing out dusky and weird amid the desolate hills. As the outline grew stronger and clearer, he rubbed his eager eyes for fear it was an enchanted vision which deceived him. But no; this surely is the solitary castle that he has so vainly sought all these long months, for it finally stands out near and distinct, and his joy is so great that he trembles in eagerness. All is as dismally quiet as of yore; and the drawbridge offering the same hospitality, he quickly rides to the entrance and is met by the silent servitor, who remembers him, and who conducts him as he did on his first visit to the great hall. Here he finds everything unchanged. The venerable Amfortas lies suffering on his bed of pain, and the ladies, knights and priests are still bound in that trance-like sleep. Once more he hears a faint murmur of chanted harmonies, the air is filled with soft light, and he witnesses the sacred procession of the veiled Grail. This time, softened by his own sufferings and overcome by heart-felt pity, he falls on his knees and cries out in anguish: —

"What ails thee, O sorrowful king? and what mean all these wondrous things?"

With these words instantly and miraculously the spell is broken. Light and life break forth through all the court, the king is healed of his long illness, the priests, knights and ladies open wide their eyes, and all are moved into waking life.

The grateful king lifted up his head and said: —

"Sir Galahad, knight and saviour! ye be most welcome, for in pain and agony have I, and all this afflicted court, long waited your coming. I trust God, now that the time has come when my pain is allayed, that I shall make my peace with heaven and be permitted to go out of this world, as was promised me so long ago."

The youthful knight came close to the side of the aged king and tenderly folded his arms about the wasted form. So hand in hand the passing king tells him of many things and instructs him in all the sacred mysteries it is so necessary for him to know as he appoints him,— the last of his own line, as they are both of the House of David,— to be his royal successor and at his death keeper of the sacred cup.

Galahad sank down on his knees by the couch and prayed long for himself and for the dying king. With the waning light came Amfortas' heart's desire, and his penitent soul, cleansed of all shame and agony, is freed at last from its tired body.

Galahad's good work is done, and his adventures here are at an end. He is free now to assume guardianship of the Holy Grail, which is to be taken from the desecrated castle which has been its home so long, and, guarded by an angel, carried across the sea to the Holy Land. He is now assured of the achievement of his holy mission, but the end is still farther on; again mounting his faithful charger he turns toward the sea, which he is to cross.

Peace and plenty abound in the formerly stricken country, now green and blossoming into freshness on every side. The wondrous substance of the Grail gleaming and glowing in the sweet air as the angel bears it away from the castle penetrates every nook and corner with its brightness, redeeming the whole land. She who was the Loathely Maiden and her companions basking in its rays, are once more beautiful in form and feature. The sorrowful lesson of their long and hateful servitude has purified them of their selfish pleasures, and they will now do good in the world instead of evil. As he rides through the joyous land upon this his last great adventure, he is greeted on every side by the thankful people, who bless him and cry with one accord: —

"Peace be with you, Fair Lord! May God give thee joy and good adventure."

A new-born spiritual enlightenment thrills his very being, begotten by his knowledge of that which his exalted responsibility entails, and gladly renouncing every human tie in the happiness of his royal guardianship, he follows the Holy Grail to its last abiding place on earth.

Night and day he rides, until at noon of the third day he comes to the sea-port. Here he finds a wonderful ship at anchor and his two brother-knights, Sir Launcelot and Sir Bors, waiting for him on the shore. These two noble knights are to be allowed to accompany Sir Galahad on this his last journey, as they have been faithful in their fruitless search, and although the object of their vow has been almost within their grasp, for the sin of one slight imperfection they have failed, as the Holy Grail is a searcher of hearts and cannot be deceived. But their honor and faithfulness have earned for them the right to witness the great achievement of their more worthy comrade.

On meeting they embrace each other, and exchanging greetings embark on the vessel, which lies in the quiet harbor. This ship, so marvelously wrought, had been built long years ago by wise old king Solomon for his own use. But when it was finished and he was about to go on board, it was made manifest to him by an angel, that it should not be used by him, or any man, until a "good knight" should come, who would be the last in the line of royal succession and whose destiny it was to be conducted by this ship to a great city on an island. So king Solomon drew back and dared not enter the ship, and it had not been used, but miraculously preserved through all these scores of years for this very purpose.

They find the angel in charge of the covered Grail sitting in the bow of the ship, and as they spread the silken sails to the favoring wind they see on their snowy surface a bright-red cross exactly like the one borne on Galahad's shield.

Fearlessly putting forth the frail vessel, with its gleaming sails, on the great waves of the mighty deep, it rides the white crests like a sea bird, under the faithful guidance of the angel. Unconscious of the days as they pass, never feeling cold or hungry, the Holy Grail being always with them, they are carried on their journey across the great sea in perfect safety.

One early morning just as day was breaking

through the sky they caught a glint of the sun as it touched the silvery turrets and shining domes that rose above the misty line of a shore and knew that their voyage was over and that they were safely in the port of the "Spiritual City."

As they entered the harbor the people ran down along the shore to meet the ship, and recognizing the cross, which was borne on the sail, and Galahad's shield as belonging to Evelac, received them as holy men. This very shield is their traditional heritage, as it had belonged to the one who had ruled their city in olden days and whose memory they had been taught to love and revere. It was he who had carried it in a famous battle and by its invulnerable power had conquered a nation.

Galahad and the two knights were conducted to the presence of the ruling king and were made welcome at the castle and shown great honor.

By the love of God there was a power conferred upon Galahad for his purity and of his holy office, enabling him to do many miracles among the poor, healing the sick and providing for those in need. Most of his time he devoted to this service of God in giving himself unselfishly in these acts of charity and kindness to his fellowmen, and the wicked king became very jealous of his popularity among the people. So fearful did his rage become in consternation at his own waning influence and power that he seized Sir Galahad and his two companions and shut them up in a deep hole in the city prison with the intention that they should die there of starvation. But the Holy Grail came to them in their dungeon and ministered to them as it had to Joseph of Arimathea, Galahad's saintly ancestor, and they were preserved through its wondrous substance.

At last the wicked king and tyrant fell ill, and on his death-bed repenting of his evil deed he sent a message to the three knights of the Grail imploring them to come to his bed-side that he might crave their forgiveness for the insults and injuries he had heaped on their blameless heads. This they gladly did and freely forgave him, and when the penitent king had died, by the assent of the whole city, Galahad was chosen his successor, and so came to his kingship.

His first act as king was to build on a hill a beautiful temple, which he called the "Sacred Place," where the guardian angel, who had tenderly cared for the Grail since it came in the ship, deposited the Holy Treasure, which was to be its last resting place on earth.

To this source of glory and wisdom the good knights came every morning and evening to offer up their prayers and adoration. One night while kneeling before the altar Galahad prayed aloud to God that he might be permitted to pass out of this world when he should ask it. And a voice answered: —

"Galahad, thou shalt have thy desire. And when thou asketh the death of thy body, then thou shalt find the life eternal of thy soul."

The other knights wondered that he should make this request, and asked him: —

"Why desirest thou this above all other favors?" And he answered them, saying: —

"In one of the holy services in which the sacred cup was used, I felt such joy as never mortal felt before. This I am sure is what the angels know every moment in heaven, and for that reason I long to be among them, now that my earthly mission is fulfilled."

On the last day of the year in which Galahad had reigned over the Holy City, he rose very early in the morning, and rousing Sir Launcelot and Sir Bors, the three came together to the "Sacred Place." After the sacrament had been celebrated Galahad continued kneeling before the altar, and lifting up his voice cried aloud for the fulfillment of his great desire.

"Now, Blessed Lord and Saviour, would I not longer live. If it please Thee, grant my prayer, for I would be in heaven with Thee."

In this mighty moment crown, scepter and robe fall from him, as he no longer needs earthly glory, and, lifting up his eyes, Galahad the pure, having through all ordeals remained sinless, beholds the Holy Grail in its unveiled glory, which no man might look upon and live.

The great achievement is his, and his soul stainless as when it came into the world, is borne to heaven by a host of angels, who fold their wings with loving reverence around the golden cup of the Holy Grail, and it is carried away with him to the clouds, never to be seen on earth again.

When all was done Sir Launcelot and Sir Bors traveled night and day as fast as they could till they came to Camelot to tell king Arthur the last of the happenings to the Holy Grail, which he had set down in writing.